AF575870

This journal belongs to:

Parks and Recreation

The Treat Yo' Self

Guided Journal

A Year of Self-Care

INSIGHT
EDITIONS

San Rafael Los Angeles London

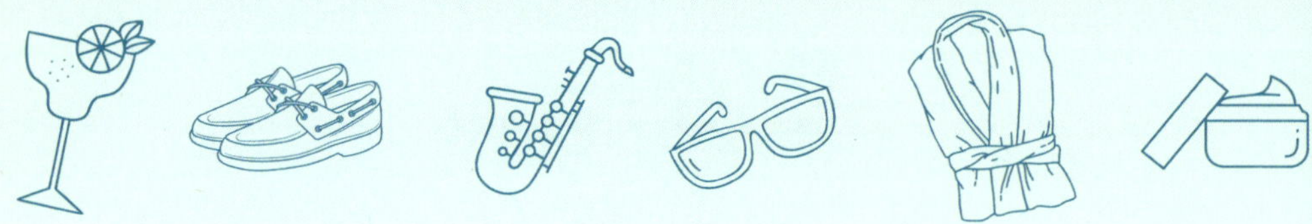

Every year, Donna Meagle and Tom Haverford treat themselves to a wide array of stunning indulgences.

Because you can't regularly splurge as if every day were Treat Yo' Self Day, you might find small ways to practice self-care regularly. Doing something special for yourself is an essential aspect of any self-care practice. For example, you might set aside time every day to engage in a simple, relaxing, and fun activity, such as reading a book with some morning coffee. That is just one way to treat yo' self on a regular basis, while also building a great self-care routine.

Self-care routines are unique to every individual, but for many, self-care involves relaxing activities, such as reading a book, as well as having healthy eating habits, getting a regular amount of sleep, and maintaining some form of movement. No matter how you choose to define self-care, it is important that you establish routines and practices to help you recharge. Remember, self-care isn't a bad thing. You are not selfish for wanting to be the best person you can be!

So, get ready to treat yo' self! This guided journal, filled with fifty-two weeks of prompts, will inspire you to regularly treat yo' self while building good self-care practices.

You will also be guided to reflect on a myriad of other feel-good topics ranging from self-compassion to finding inspiration in the gleaming beacon of radiance that is Li'l Sebastian.

There are two types of writing activities for each week:

The first offers space for simple "one-line-a-day" journaling, allowing you to record moments of self-care daily. You may not have the opportunity to experience these types of moments every day, and that's okay. When life gets busy, use the space provided to journal about any topic that feels right to you in the moment—even if it's just a favorite memory of *Parks and Recreation*!

The second calls for deeper reflection through freewriting, list-making, coloring, and other activities. These prompts will also help you to initiate and complete fun and meaningful goals, such as volunteer work and kind acts for your friends and family.

As you embark on your year of self-care, just remember that you're worth it. Treat yo' self! You deserve it.

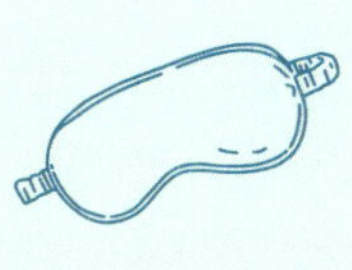

DAILY MOMENTS OF SELF-CARE

Monday

Tuesday

Wednesday

Thursday

Friday

Saturday

Sunday

Treat Yo' Self

“Clothes?”

“Treat yo’ self.”

“Fragrances?”

“Treat yo’ self.”

“Massages?”

“Treat yo’ self.”

“Mimosas?”

“Treat yo’ self.”

“Fine leather goods?”

“Treat yo’ self.”

“It’s the best day of the year!”

–Donna Meagle and Tom Haverford

What is your ideal Treat Yo’ Self Day? Make a list of activities that you would do during your own Treat Yo’ Self Day. If you need some inspiration, look no further than Donna and Tom—we see them go on a Hollywood bus tour and get their elbows bedazzled with diamonds. The sky is the limit!

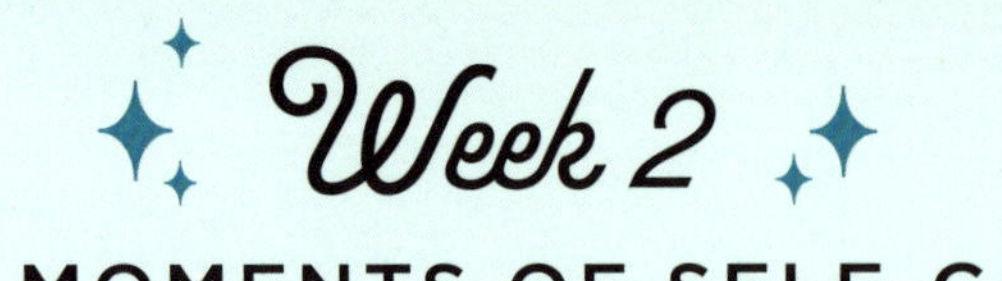

DAILY MOMENTS OF SELF-CARE

Monday

Tuesday

Wednesday

Thursday

Friday

Saturday

Sunday

TREAT YO' SELF

Week 2

Donna and Tom blow big money on Treat Yo' Self Day, but you don't need to spend money to pamper yourself or build elaborate self-care practices.

What are some inexpensive—even free—ways that you can treat yo' self? You might take a walk in the park, listen to some music, or spend time with a friend.

Week 3

DAILY MOMENTS OF SELF-CARE

Monday

Tuesday

Wednesday

Thursday

Friday

Saturday

Sunday

Treat Yo' Self

Week 3

But . . . if you could blow big money on one thing, what would it be, and why?

Week 4

DAILY MOMENTS OF SELF-CARE

Monday

Tuesday

Wednesday

Thursday

Friday

Saturday

Sunday

Treat Yo' Self

Week 4

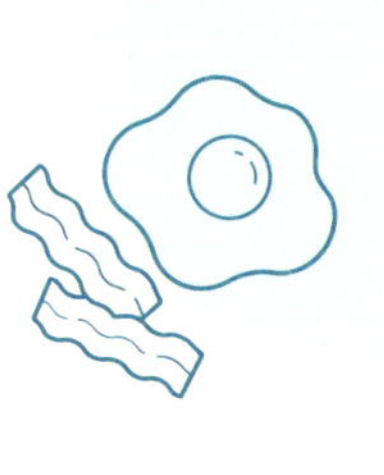

“Fishing relaxes me. It's like yoga, except I still get to kill something.”
—Ron Swanson

Sometimes, treating yo' self simply means doing something fun and relaxing. Not only is relaxing a way to treat yo' self, but it's also a critical form of self-care.

What relaxes you? List some relaxation activities below and write about why you consider them a form of self-care.

Week 5

DAILY MOMENTS OF SELF-CARE

Monday

Tuesday

Wednesday

Thursday

Friday

Saturday

Sunday

TREAT YO' SELF

Week 5

"Ann, you poetic, noble land-mermaid."
—Leslie Knope

Leslie has a never-ending series of positive affirmations for her best friend, Ann, referring to her as a "beautiful, rule-breaking moth," a "beautiful tropical starfish," and a "beautiful, talented, brilliant, powerful musk ox."

As a way of practicing self-compassion, create positive affirmations addressed to yourself, in the style of Leslie Knope. Then, come up with additional affirmations to send to someone who might need a pick-me-up.

Week 6

DAILY MOMENTS OF SELF-CARE

Monday

Tuesday

Wednesday

Thursday

Friday

Saturday

Sunday

Treat Yo' Self

Week 6

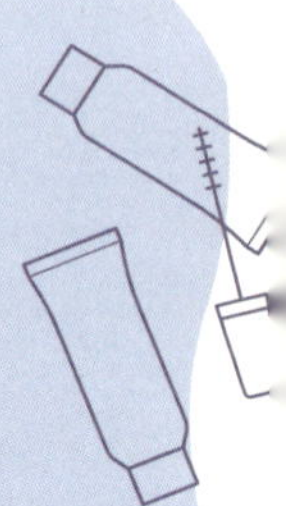

Treating yo' self to nice things is important, but it is equally important to be grateful for the positive elements of your present life. Gratitude is a helpful aspect of any self-care practice, because it helps relieve anxiety and allows you to reflect on what you have, rather than fixate on what you don't.

Following up on last week's prompt, is there someone in your life you are grateful for? Reflect on why you are grateful for them in the space below!

DAILY MOMENTS OF SELF-CARE

Monday

Tuesday

Wednesday

Thursday

Friday

Saturday

Sunday

Treat Yo' Self

Week 7

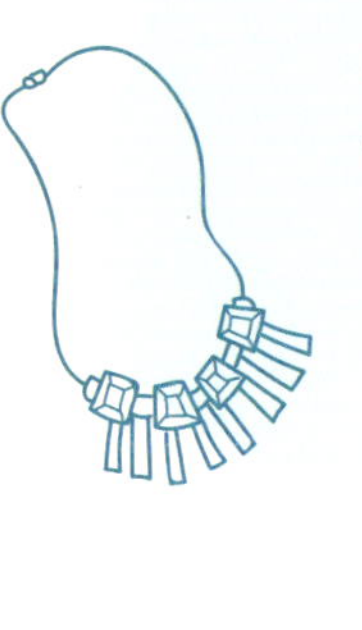

Treat the B-words (buddies!) in your life. When Donna and Tom saw Ben struggling with stress, they threw him in Donna's car and included him in Treat Yo' Self Day.

Is there someone in your life who could benefit from a day of pampering? Plan a Treat Yo' Self Day for a loved one below. Bonus points if you actually have a Treat Yo' Self Day together!

DAILY MOMENTS OF SELF-CARE

Monday

Tuesday

Wednesday

Thursday

Friday

Saturday

Sunday

Treat Yo' Self

Week 8

Spending time outdoors is a great way to practice self-care. Take a walk today, or simply sit outside and notice the things around you. Try to be mindful and present in the moment.

Write about the things you saw, the sounds you heard, and how you felt upon returning home. Just remember, if you see any raccoons like Fairway Frank, call Pawnee Animal Control.

DAILY MOMENTS OF SELF-CARE

Monday

Tuesday

Wednesday

Thursday

Friday

Saturday

Sunday

Treat Yo' Self

“I am a goddess, a glorious female warrior. Queen of all that I survey. Enemies of fairness and equality, hear my womanly roar.”
—The Pawnee Goddesses pledge

If you formed a troop similar to Leslie’s Pawnee Goddesses and Ron’s Pawnee Rangers, what would the pledge be? Brainstorm some ideas in the space below!

Week 10

DAILY MOMENTS OF SELF-CARE

Monday

Tuesday

Wednesday

Thursday

Friday

Saturday

Sunday

Treat Yo' Self

Week 10

“When I started working for you, I was aimless and just thought everything was stupid and lame . . . and you turned me into someone with goals and ambition.”
—April Ludgate to Leslie Knope

Who are some mentors in your life who have impacted you in a positive way? How can you be a mentor to others in your life?

DAILY MOMENTS OF SELF-CARE

Monday

Tuesday

Wednesday

Thursday

Friday

Saturday

Sunday

Treat Yo' Self

Week 11

"Never half-ass two things. Whole-ass one thing."
—Ron Swanson

PRIORITY

Is there a task that you have been putting off? Build up your sense of self-trust by getting it done! Write about a short-term goal you have and how you can achieve it.

DAILY MOMENTS OF SELF-CARE

Monday

Tuesday

Wednesday

Thursday

Friday

Saturday

Sunday

Treat Yo' Self

Week 12

"Pawnee's Library Department is the most diabolical ruthless bunch of bureaucrats I've ever seen. They're like a biker gang. But instead of shotguns and crystal meth, they use political savvy and shushing."
—Leslie Knope

Even though Leslie has much disdain for the librarians of Pawnee, there's no denying that settling down with a good book is one of the top five ways to treat yo' self. (It's right in between buying a full-sized Batsuit and dining on sushi made with fish that was previously owned by celebrities.)

What are some books that are meaningful to you? Could you treat yo' self to some reading time this week?

DAILY MOMENTS OF SELF-CARE

Monday

Tuesday

Wednesday

Thursday

Friday

Saturday

Sunday

Treat Yo' Self

Week 13

“There’s something about the sound of harps that makes me nervous.”
—Ben Wyatt

As a relaxation novice, Ben has a hard time getting used to the pampering of Donna and Tom’s Treat Yo’ Self Day, especially at the spa.

What are some things that others might treat themselves to that you don’t particularly enjoy? What are some things that you like to do that are unique to you?

Week 14

DAILY MOMENTS OF SELF-CARE

Monday

Tuesday

Wednesday

Thursday

Friday

Saturday

Sunday

TREAT YO' SELF

Week 14

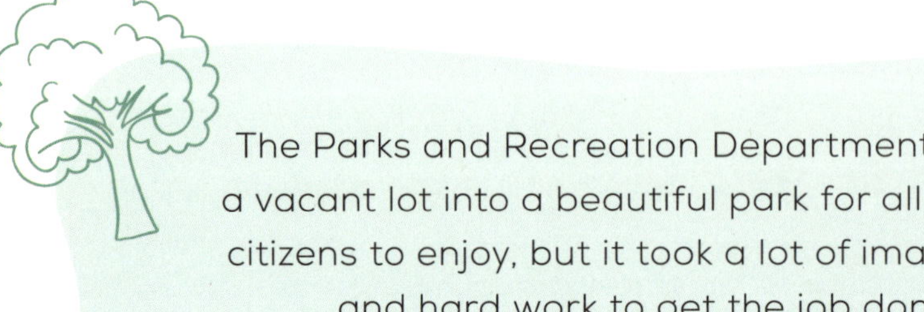

The Parks and Recreation Department turned a vacant lot into a beautiful park for all Pawnee citizens to enjoy, but it took a lot of imagination and hard work to get the job done.

Is there a personal space or object that you could transform into something beautiful? How would you achieve it?

Week 15

DAILY MOMENTS OF SELF-CARE

Monday

Tuesday

Wednesday

Thursday

Friday

Saturday

Sunday

Treat Yo' Self

Week 15

Pawnee's great treasure, Li'l Sebastian, lived a storied life. His many travels took him to England, Kuwait, and beyond.

Are there places you dream of visiting in your life? Write about them below.

Week 16

DAILY MOMENTS OF SELF-CARE

Monday

Tuesday

Wednesday

Thursday

Friday

Saturday

Sunday

Treat Yo' Self

Week 16

When Ron and Chris attended a meditation class, Ron was able to easily quiet his mind, while Chris had a hard time doing so. As a form of self-care, meditation is a great way to treat yo' self!

Meditation might not always be easy, but it is often worth the effort, as it can help you relax and be mindful. Find a comfortable seat in a quiet area. Set a timer for a few minutes—one to five minutes should suffice, as meditation doesn't need to be a lengthy activity to help you feel grounded and present.

Close your eyes and breathe deeply. After the timer goes off, open your eyes, and write about how you feel.

Week 17

DAILY MOMENTS OF SELF-CARE

Monday

Tuesday

Wednesday

Thursday

Friday

Saturday

Sunday

Treat Yo' Self

Week 17

When Leslie was recalled from the City Council, she thought that she had lost her dream job. But like Jennifer Barkley noted, losing that job was in Leslie's favor, and she used the experience to go on to bigger and better things.

Have you ever experienced a similar event? Write about a time in your life when a failure became a positive experience. How did you get past any negative feelings that arose during that situation?

DAILY MOMENTS OF SELF-CARE

Monday

Tuesday

Wednesday

Thursday

Friday

Saturday

Sunday

TREAT YO' SELF

Week 18

“Jogging is the worst, Chris. I mean, I know it keeps you healthy, but God, at what cost?”
—Ann Perkins

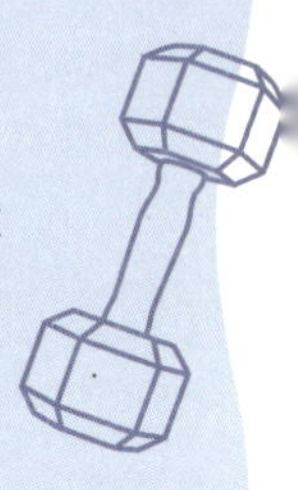

Chris goes on runs to get his endorphins going, but any kind of physical activity can get your heart pumping and improve your mood. In fact, regular movement is one of the best forms of self-care there is, no matter how small!

Do you have a favorite physical activity? How does it *literally* make you feel?

Week 19

DAILY MOMENTS OF SELF-CARE

Monday

Tuesday

Wednesday

Thursday

Friday

Saturday

Sunday

TREAT YO' SELF

Week 19

“Anything is possible if you follow your dreams.”
—Johnny Karate

Do you have goals that you want to accomplish this month? Within the year? Write about them below. Now create a plan to make your goals happen. Spread your wings and fly!

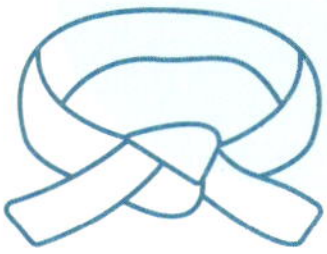

DAILY MOMENTS OF SELF-CARE

Monday

Tuesday

Wednesday

Thursday

Friday

Saturday

Sunday

Treat Yo' Self

Week 20

Ben created the Cones of Dunshire gaming experience during a week off of work. Brilliant ideas, creations, and solutions often come from giving yourself space to indulge your hobbies.

As we all know, doing a fun and relaxing activity is a great way to treat yo' self and recharge. Explore whatever fun activity pops into your brain today, and write about it below.

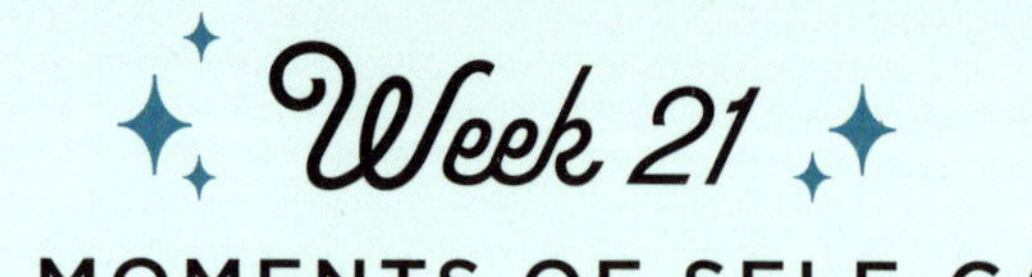

Week 21

DAILY MOMENTS OF SELF-CARE

Monday

Tuesday

Wednesday

Thursday

Friday

Saturday

Sunday

TREAT YO' SELF

Week 21

Donna and Tom are two characters who have a good sense of their own self-worth. They see themselves as people who are worthy of love and some indulgence, here and there.

Have the previous twenty weeks of journaling helped you to treat yo' self and practice self-care? Reflect on your self-care journey as you color in the scene on the opposite page.

Then, decorate the following spread with illustrations, taped- or glued-in ephemera, or other embellishments that represent your self-care journey so far.

"Treat yo' self"

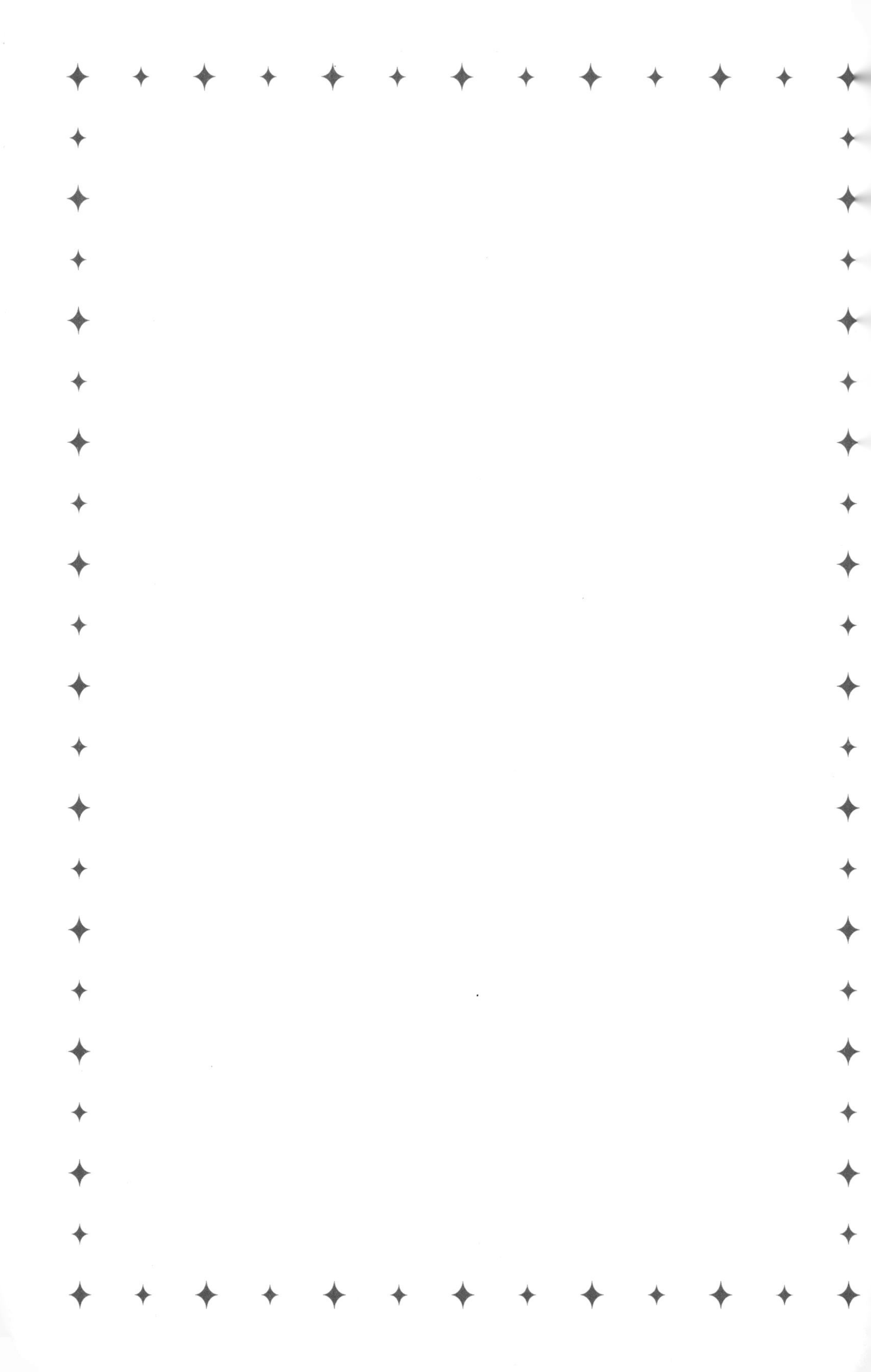

Week 22

DAILY MOMENTS OF SELF-CARE

Monday

Tuesday

Wednesday

Thursday

Friday

Saturday

Sunday

Treat Yo' Self

Week 22

“[Dogs] should be rewarded for not being people. I hate people.”
—April Ludgate

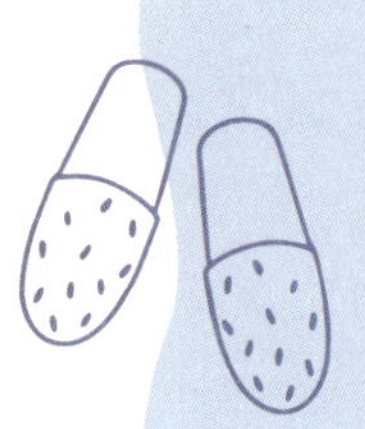

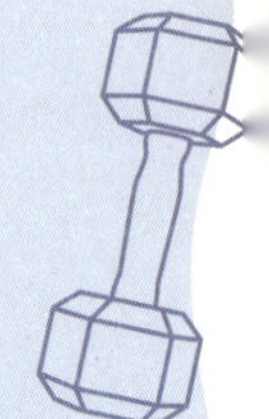

Pets are known to bring a great deal of emotional benefits, such as stress relief, as well as physical benefits, as any owner of an energetic dog knows!

Do you have any pets in your life? What is one thing that you can do to treat yo' self and your pet together? If you don't have any pets, what would your ideal pet be?

DAILY MOMENTS OF SELF-CARE

Monday

Tuesday

Wednesday

Thursday

Friday

Saturday

Sunday

Treat Yo' Self

Week 23

"I am calm. I am grateful. I am Craig."
—Craig Middlebrooks

With the help of Dr. Richard Nygard, Craig develops methods of staying calm during stressful situations.

Try repeating some of the phrases below when you encounter stress. Write down some of your own as well.

"I am calm and relaxed."
"I am brave."
"I am strong."
"I am resilient."
"I am capable of achieving my dreams."

DAILY MOMENTS OF SELF-CARE

Monday

Tuesday

Wednesday

Thursday

Friday

Saturday

Sunday

Treat Yo' Self

Week 24

"I am big enough to admit I am often inspired by myself."
—Leslie Knope

Don't be afraid to admit it! What have you done or said or created that was so amazing that even you were impressed?

Week 25

DAILY MOMENTS OF SELF-CARE

Monday

Tuesday

Wednesday

Thursday

Friday

Saturday

Sunday

Treat Yo' Self

Week 25

Do you need a break from work or school, or even a few hours to yourself? Treat yo' self to a mental health day! For Ron, this might involve paddling a canoe in a peaceful lake, whereas Andy might have a jam session with his bandmates.

What are some things you can do to recharge?

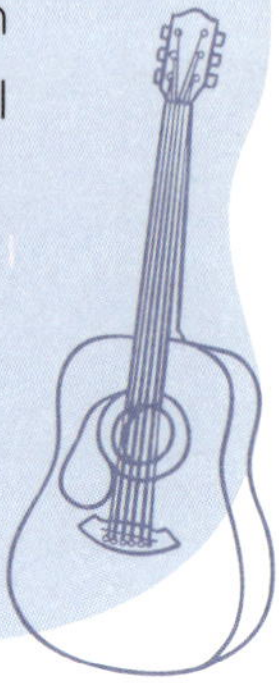

DAILY MOMENTS OF SELF-CARE

Monday

Tuesday

Wednesday

Thursday

Friday

Saturday

Sunday

Treat Yo' Self

When Andy returns to college, Ron encourages him to learn, explore a new subject, and broaden his horizons.

Challenge yourself to do one new thing this week, and record how it went in the space provided.

Week 27

DAILY MOMENTS OF SELF-CARE

Monday

Tuesday

Wednesday

Thursday

Friday

Saturday

Sunday

Treat Yo' Self

Week 27

Leslie is challenged by a citizen named Garth Blunden to live as a Pawneean from the 1800s.

In the spirit of Garth's challenge, turn off your devices or set them to silent mode, and spend a day completely off the grid. How did it feel to be disconnected? Hopefully, you fared better than Leslie did!

Week 28

DAILY MOMENTS OF SELF-CARE

Monday

Tuesday

Wednesday

Thursday

Friday

Saturday

Sunday

Treat Yo' Self

"My mind is a steel trap of friendship nuggets."
—Leslie Knope

Leslie gives amazing gifts to her friends because she knows them so well! What is something nice that you can do for a loved one? Use the space below to plan an unexpected, yet perfect treat for someone in your life.

Week 29

DAILY MOMENTS OF SELF-CARE

Monday

Tuesday

Wednesday

Thursday

Friday

Saturday

Sunday

Treat Yo' Self

Week 29

At eighteen years old, Ben Wyatt bankrupted his hometown of Partridge, Minnesota, and was impeached within two months. Failure can help us learn about ourselves and inspire us to strive to do better in the future.

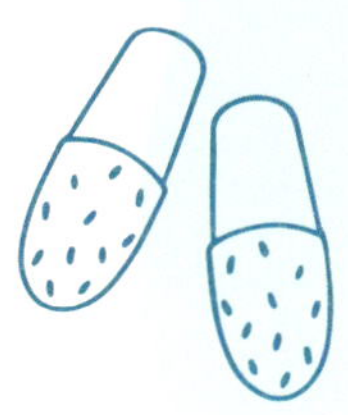

Write about a time when you failed and how you learned from your mistakes. Remember that a major component of self-care is treating yourself with kindness!

Week 30

DAILY MOMENTS OF SELF-CARE

Monday

Tuesday

Wednesday

Thursday

Friday

Saturday

Sunday

Treat Yo' Self

Week 30

“I am 100% certain that
I am 0% sure of what I’m going to do.”
–Chris Traeger

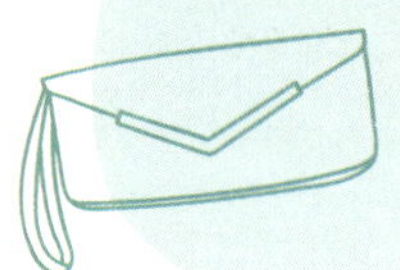

No one has all the answers, not even Chris Traeger. Write about a time when you felt lost. Were you able to overcome uncertainty? What did you learn from the experience?

Week 31

DAILY MOMENTS OF SELF-CARE

Monday

Tuesday

Wednesday

Thursday

Friday

Saturday

Sunday

Week 31

“There has never been a sadness that can't be cured by breakfast food.”
—Ron Swanson

Do you have a go-to comfort food? Write about how that indulgent/satisfying dish makes you feel comforted, or record your favorite recipe.

Then, treat yo' self to waffles (or a breakfast treat of your choice)! Use the following recipe to create a breakfast meal that Leslie Knope would approve of.

Leslie's Favorite Waffles

Serves 4 to 6
Prep time: 10 minutes
Cook time: 5 minutes per waffle

2 cups all-purpose flour

1 teaspoon kosher salt

4 teaspoons baking powder

2 tablespoons sugar

2 large eggs

1½ cups whole milk, warmed

⅓ cup butter, melted

1 teaspoon pure vanilla extract

Toppings: Whipped cream (one can for serving, and one for dispensing whipped cream directly into one's mouth), syrups of choice, assorted jams, and fresh fruit

In a bowl, whisk together flour, salt, baking powder, and sugar; set aside. Preheat waffle iron to 375°F.

In another bowl, beat the eggs. Stir in the milk, butter, and vanilla extract. Pour the milk mixture into the flour mixture; whisk gently just until blended (a few lumps are okay).

Ladle the batter into the preheated waffle iron. Cook until golden and crisp, about 5 to 6 minutes. Serve immediately with extra, extra whipped cream and other toppings.

✦ **Make it vegan:** Use equivalent amount of a plant-based egg product in place of the eggs. Substitute plant-based butter and milk for dairy butter and milk.

✦ **Make it gluten-free:** Use a gluten-free flour blend in place of the all-purpose flour.

✦ **Allergens:** Wheat, dairy

Week 32

DAILY MOMENTS OF SELF-CARE

Monday

Tuesday

Wednesday

Thursday

Friday

Saturday

Sunday

Treat Yo' Self

Just as Treat Yo' Self Day is a time-honored tradition for our favorite local government workers, so, too, is Galentine's Day!

Color in the scene on the opposite page, and reflect on the friends you would toast on Galentine's Day.

Then, decorate the following spread with illustrations, taped- or glued-in ephemera, or other embellishments that represent your best pals.

CREA

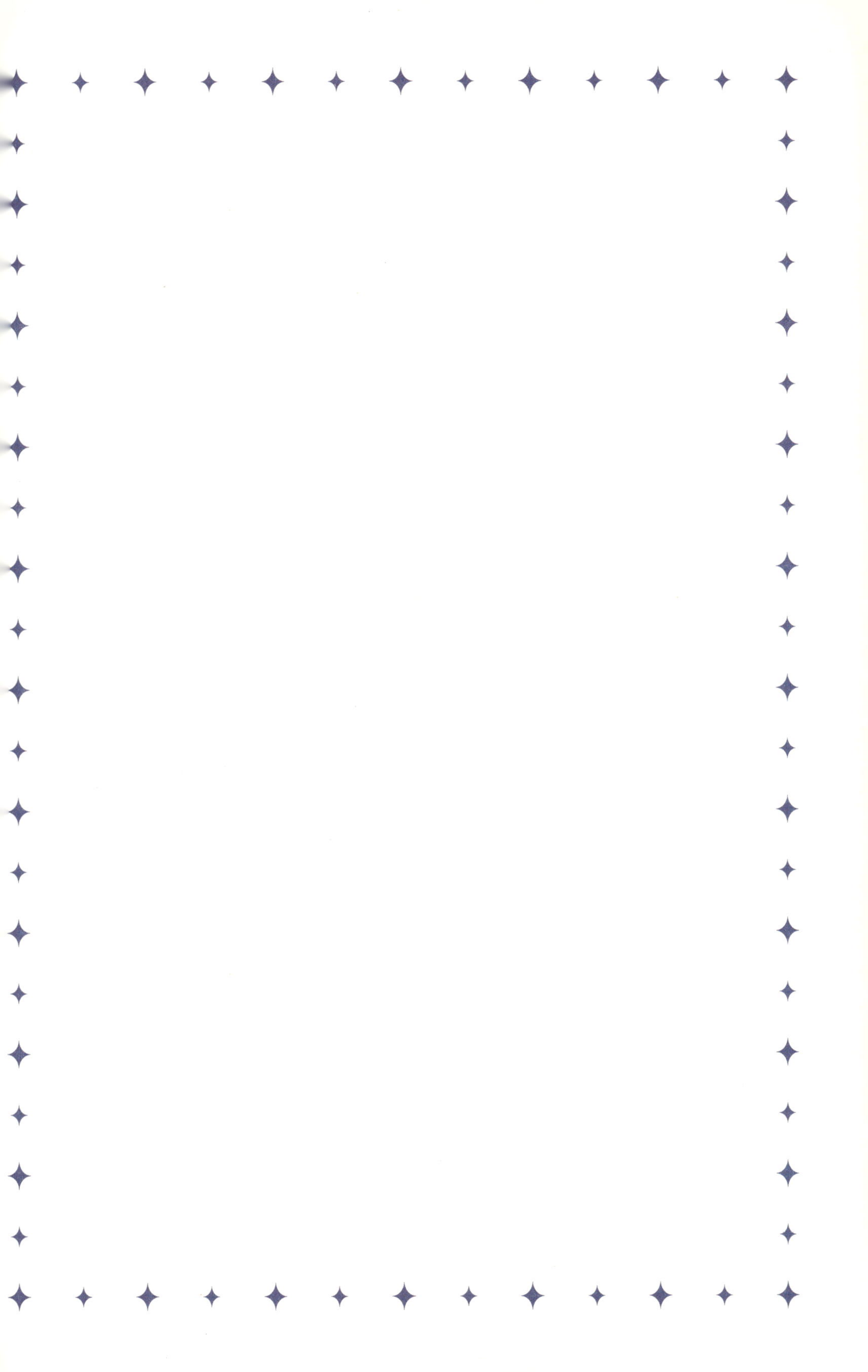

DAILY MOMENTS OF SELF-CARE

Monday

Tuesday

Wednesday

Thursday

Friday

Saturday

Sunday

Treat Yo' Self

Week 33

“She told me, ‘If you don’t love what you do . . . then why do it?’ Then she ripped the hair from my B hole.”
—Jean-Ralphio Saperstein

What are you passionate about? What is your dream job? What steps can you take to make your dream a reality? Record your thoughts in the space below.

Week 34

DAILY MOMENTS OF SELF-CARE

Monday

Tuesday

Wednesday

Thursday

Friday

Saturday

Sunday

TREAT YO' SELF

Week 34

Whether through phone banking or registering people to vote, have you been involved in politics, even locally, say, at a Parks and Recreation Department?

If an election is coming up, how might you get involved? Or is there a community that you participate in? Reflect on how you feel about being part of something greater than yourself.

Week 35

DAILY MOMENTS OF SELF-CARE

Monday

Tuesday

Wednesday

Thursday

Friday

Saturday

Sunday

Treat Yo' Self

Week 35

“We need to remember what’s important in life: friends, waffles, work. Or waffles, friends, work. Doesn’t matter, but work is third.”
—Leslie Knope

It can be difficult to prioritize relationships and self-care over work, school, or other obligations.

Write about a time when prioritizing your friends, or yourself, over other responsibilities has helped you. What can you take away from these moments?

DAILY MOMENTS OF SELF-CARE

Monday

Tuesday

Wednesday

Thursday

Friday

Saturday

Sunday

Treat Yo' Self

Chris Traeger counters negative feelings with exercise—perhaps too much, at times!

Having negative thoughts and feelings is natural, so it's important to acknowledge them without dwelling on them. What are some constructive ways that you deal with negative feelings?

Week 37

DAILY MOMENTS OF SELF-CARE

Monday

Tuesday

Wednesday

Thursday

Friday

Saturday

Sunday

Treat Yo' Self

Week 37

When Ron isn't dealing with the myriad complaints of the citizens of Pawnee, you might find him moonlighting as jazz saxophonist Duke Silver.

This week, treat yo' self to a soothing activity that brings you joy, whether it's playing tunes that are smooth as velvet, or simply coloring in the image on the opposite page.

Then, decorate the following spread with illustrations, taped- or glued-in ephemera, or other embellishments that represent your favorite ways to relax.

THE DUKE SILVER TRIO

Memories... of Now

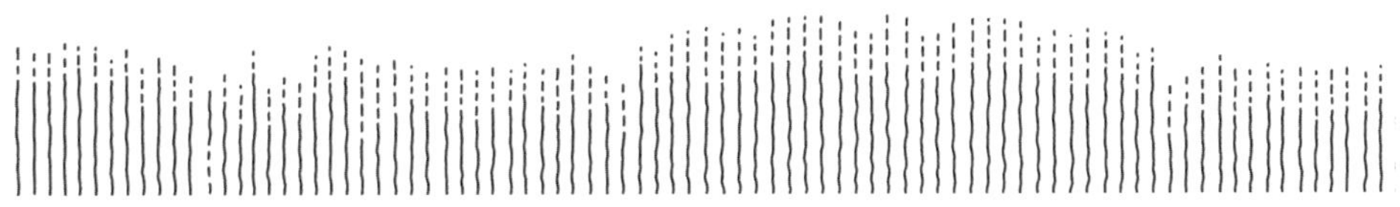

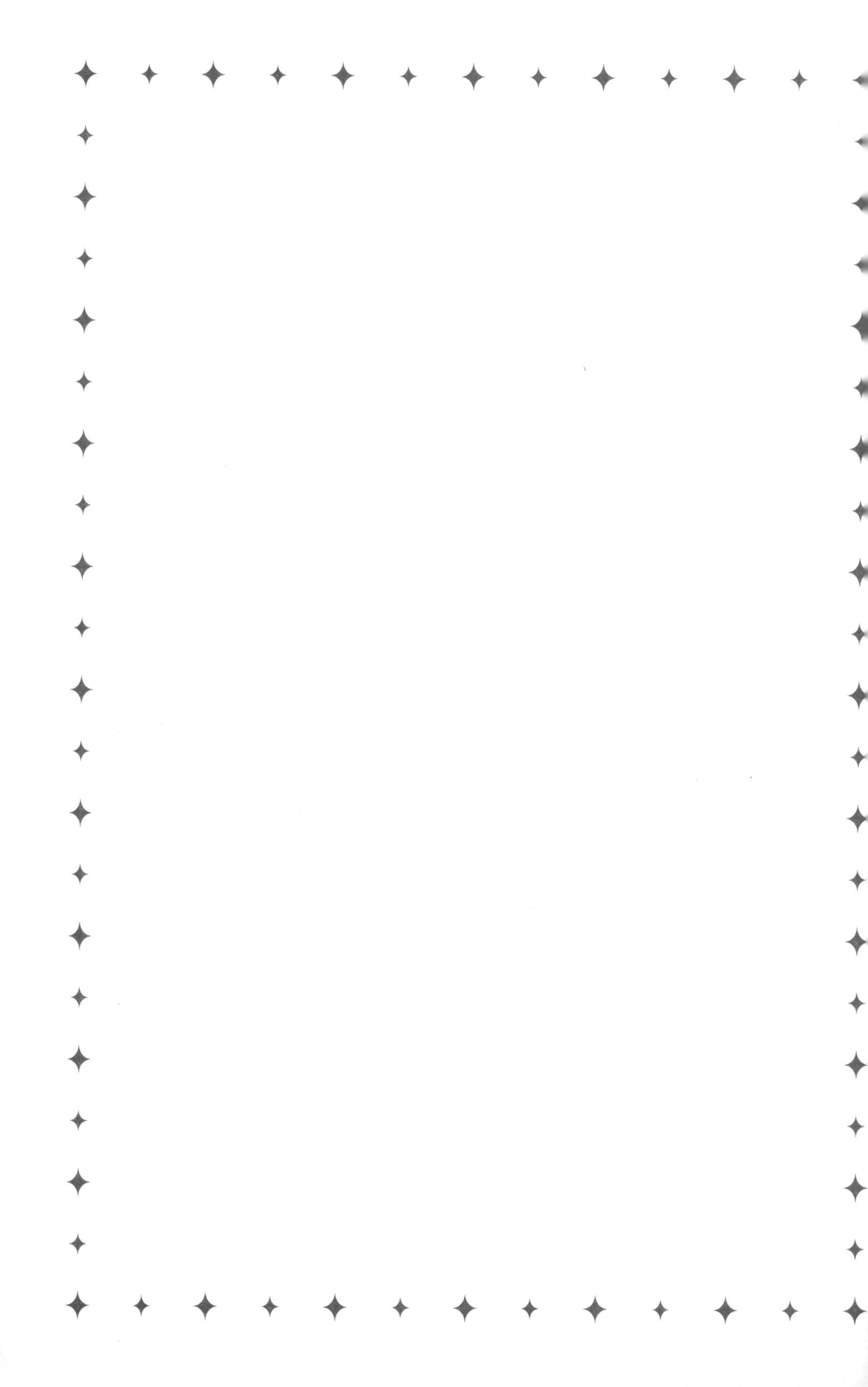

Week 38

DAILY MOMENTS OF SELF-CARE

Monday

Tuesday

Wednesday

Thursday

Friday

Saturday

Sunday

TREAT YO' SELF

Week 38

There are few things that Ron Swanson loves more than Mulligan's Steakhouse.

What was the best meal you've ever had? How can you treat yo' self to your favorite dish this week?

Week 39

DAILY MOMENTS OF SELF-CARE

Monday

Tuesday

Wednesday

Thursday

Friday

Saturday

Sunday

Treat Yo' Self

Week 39

Turn back to the very first prompt (page 6).

What is your ideal Treat Yo' Self Day? Do at least one activity from your list. Then write about what you did and how it made you feel.

DAILY MOMENTS OF SELF-CARE

Monday

Tuesday

Wednesday

Thursday

Friday

Saturday

Sunday

TREAT YO' SELF

Week 40

"Hey, Leslie. It's Leslie. Hang in there. I love you. Bye."
—Leslie Knope

Practicing self-compassion means treating yourself like you would a friend. For instance, a good friend wouldn't be too hard on you for mistakes at work or forgetting to call a loved one.

Write an encouraging letter to yourself that you can read during stressful moments. What would you say to yourself to help you through tough times?

DAILY MOMENTS OF SELF-CARE

Monday

Tuesday

Wednesday

Thursday

Friday

Saturday

Sunday

Treat Yo' Self

When Leslie becomes preoccupied with her work as a councilwoman, April must lead public forums in Leslie's stead. Despite her reservations, April eventually takes charge effectively, turning her bristly personality into her greatest strength.

Have there been times in your life when you have had to accept responsibilities that you may not have felt prepared for? Did your unique personality traits and strengths help you in those situations?

DAILY MOMENTS OF SELF-CARE

Monday

Tuesday

Wednesday

Thursday

Friday

Saturday

Sunday

TREAT YO' SELF

Week 42

“So, I just slept seven hours, which is twice as long as I usually sleep . . . so I'm a little disoriented.”
—Leslie Knope

Having a healthy amount of sleep isn't just a way to treat yo' self—it's a critical element of self-care! Try to get seven to nine hours of sleep per night this week even if you have to change your nighttime routine a bit, such as shutting down devices earlier.

How did you feel the morning after? Did you notice any improvements on your focus or creativity during the day?

Week 43

DAILY MOMENTS OF SELF-CARE

Monday

Tuesday

Wednesday

Thursday

Friday

Saturday

Sunday

Treat Yo' Self

Week 43

Whether it's Donna and Tom, Leslie and Ben, or April and Andy, our relationships—whether they're platonic or romantic—have the potential to bring out our best qualities.

Write about how a friend, romantic partner, or someone important brings out the best in you.

Week 44

DAILY MOMENTS OF SELF-CARE

Monday

Tuesday

Wednesday

Thursday

Friday

Saturday

Sunday

TREAT YO' SELF

Week 44

April and Andy drove all the way to the Grand Canyon to cross the experience off Andy's bucket list.

If you could drop everything and go on a spontaneous adventure, where would you go?

Week 45

DAILY MOMENTS OF SELF-CARE

Monday

Tuesday

Wednesday

Thursday

Friday

Saturday

Sunday

TREAT YO' SELF

Week 45

Despite their differences, the people of Pawnee and Eagleton unite—Donna's counterpart in Eagleton's Parks and Recreation Department, Craig, even joins the Pawnee crew.

Have you ever had to find common ground with someone? What happened and how did you move through it?

Week 46

DAILY MOMENTS OF SELF-CARE

Monday

Tuesday

Wednesday

Thursday

Friday

Saturday

Sunday

TREAT YO' SELF

Week 46

Follow one of the most important rules of the carefully calibrated Swanson Pyramid of Greatness:

"Give 100%. 110% is impossible. Only idiots recommend that."

Even masters at multitasking like Leslie Knope can struggle with prioritizing the Parks Department and City Council.

List your priorities for the week here and then list activities that you would like to do. How can you prioritize so you can accomplish both the priorities and a few additional activities?

Remember, one shouldn't feel bad about taking some time off to do activities that help you recharge. Rest is productive, since it helps you to be your best self!

DAILY MOMENTS OF SELF-CARE

Monday

Tuesday

Wednesday

Thursday

Friday

Saturday

Sunday

Treat Yo' Self

Week 47

Just as Andy Dwyer and April Ludgate transform into Burt Macklin and Janet Snakehole, it's time to come up with your own alter ego! Are you a karate master, the best agent the FBI ever had, or Mother Nature's brother, Brother Nature?

Come up with your own character and write about your adventures.

Week 48

DAILY MOMENTS OF SELF-CARE

Monday

Tuesday

Wednesday

Thursday

Friday

Saturday

Sunday

Week 48

Treating yourself and practicing self-care are important as a way to recharge. But the benefits of self-care can extend beyond yourself. When you're recharged, then you have the energy to take care of your loved ones and your community. The Parks and Recreation Department dedicates itself to providing the community with fun activities that bring the people of Pawnee together.

Are there ways you can engage with your own community? Look up volunteer opportunities near you, and write about your plans to do some volunteer work.

Week 49

DAILY MOMENTS OF SELF-CARE

Monday

Tuesday

Wednesday

Thursday

Friday

Saturday

Sunday

Week 49

“I love you and I like you.”
—Leslie Knope.

What are five things that you love about yourself? Treat yo’ self to some kind words!

Week 50

DAILY MOMENTS OF SELF-CARE

Monday

Tuesday

Wednesday

Thursday

Friday

Saturday

Sunday

Treat Yo' Self

Week 50

What were the goals that you accomplished this year? Were they short-term or long-term? If life got in the way of some things, don't be too hard on yourself! Are there goals you'd like to carry into the next year?

Week 51

DAILY MOMENTS OF SELF-CARE

Monday

Tuesday

Wednesday

Thursday

Friday

Saturday

Sunday

Treat Yo' Self

Week 51

As your first Treat Yo' Self year comes to an end, reflect on what you have learned about pampering yourself, relaxing, and making time for yourself. How have you grown? What things remain to be learned?

DAILY MOMENTS OF SELF-CARE

Monday

Tuesday

Wednesday

Thursday

Friday

Saturday

Sunday

Treat Yo' Self

Week 52

“For the last time, and I won't say this again, there will be no human or feline ashes in either one of the time capsules.”
—Leslie Knope

Write about your life right now. This could be anything—simple notes, such as what music you're listening to, or deep reflections on your current state of mind.

Keep this journal in a safe place so you can find it again and look back on your old self. Think of this journal as a time capsule. Throughout next year, remember to treat yo' self to days of rest and reflection regularly!

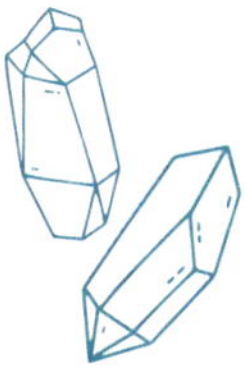

PO Box 3088 San Rafael, CA 94912
www.insighteditions.com

Find us on Facebook: www.facebook.com/InsightEditions
Follow us on Twitter: @insighteditions

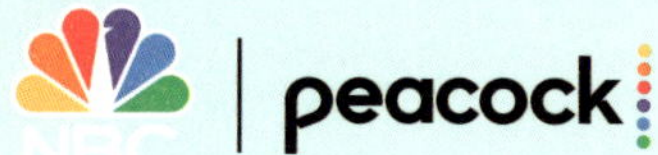

Published by Insight Editions, San Rafael, California, in 2022.

Library of Congress Cataloging-in-Publication Data available.
ISBN: 978-1-64722-673-2

Publisher: Raoul Goff
VP of Licensing and Partnerships: Vanessa Lopez
VP of Creative: Chrissy Kwasnik
VP of Manufacturing: Alix Nicholaeff
VP, Editorial Director: Vicki Jaeger
Art Director: Ashley Quackenbush
Production Designer: Amy Tang
Editor: Harrison Tunggal
Senior Production Editor: Katie Rokakis
Managing Editor: Maria Spano
Production Associate: Tiffani Patterson
Senior Production Manager, Subsidiary Rights: Lina s Palma-Temena

Text by Elizabeth Ovieda and Harrison Tunggal
Illustrations on pages 87, 135, and 157 by Valentin Ramon.

Insight Editions, in association with Roots of Peace, will plant two trees for each tree used in the manufacturing of this book. Roots of Peace is an internationally renowned humanitarian organization dedicated to eradicating land mines worldwide and converting war-torn lands into productive farms and wildlife habitats. Roots of Peace will plant two million fruit and nut trees in Afghanistan and provide farmers there with the skills and support necessary for sustainable land use.

Manufactured in China by Insight Editions

10 9 8 7 6 5 4 3 2 1